Warren Chase

**The American Crisis**

Trial and triumph of Democracy

Warren Chase

**The American Crisis**
*Trial and triumph of Democracy*

ISBN/EAN: 9783337378677

Printed in Europe, USA, Canada, Australia, Japan

Cover: Foto ©Andreas Hilbeck / pixelio.de

More available books at **www.hansebooks.com**

# THE AMERICAN CRISIS;

OR,

# TRIAL AND TRIUMPH OF DEMOCRACY.

BY WARREN CHASE,

AUTHOR OF "LIFE LINE OF THE LONE ONE," "FUGITIVE WIFE," ETC.

"War is the statesman's game, the lawyer's jest,
The priest's delight, and the hired assassin's trade."
SHELLEY.

We will defend the government that secures to all its children land, labor, and education.

BOSTON:

PUBLISHED BY BELA MARSH,

14 BROMFIELD STREET.

Stereotyped by
HOBART & ROBBINS,
New England Type and Stereotype Foundery,
BOSTON.

# CONTENTS.

# INTRODUCTION.

If this little work needs an introduction, it may be given in few words. It is the friend to the working man and woman, and the defence of true democracy,—showing the part they take, and the interest they have, in the American Rebellion of 1861 and 1862. Should it chance to fall into the hands of an aristocrat, he or she is kindly requested by the author to hand it to the hired man or woman.

# THE AMERICAN CRISIS.

## MEN OF ACTION, CLEAR THE WAY.

BY CHARLES MACKAY.

MEN of thought, be up and stirring,
 Night and day ;
Sow the seed, withdraw the curtain,
 Clear the way !
Men of action aid and cheer them
 As you may.
There is a fount about to stream,
There is a light about to beam,
There is a warmth about to glow,
There is a flower about to blow,
There is a midnight darkness
. Changing into gray.
Men of thought, and men of action,
 *Clear the way!*

Once the welcome light has broken, —
 Who shall say
What the unimagined glories
 Of the day ?
What the evil that shall perish
 In its ray ? *
Aid the dawning tongue and pen ;
Aid it, hopes of honest men ;
Aid it, paper ; aid it, type ;
Aid it, for the hour is ripe,

1*        (5)

And our earnest must not slacken　　•
    Into play.
Men of thought, and men of action,
    *Clear the way!*

Lo ! a cloud 's about to vanish
    From the day ;
And a brazen wrong to crumble
    Into clay,
Lo ! the right 's about to conquer :
    *Clear the way !*
With the right shall many more
Enter smiling at the door ;
With the giant wrong shall fall --
Many others, great and small,
That for ages long have held us
    For their prey.
Men of thought and men of action,
    *Clear the way !*

As no prophecy, to my knowledge, has reached this era, or described this evil, therefore I have no fulfilment to describe, but only to delineate, simply and plainly, causes, effects and prospects, as they appear to persons who look up principles as causes for effects.

Every future reader of American history will be able to point out this war, which broke out in 1861, between the cotton and the corn States, as the trial of strength for democratic government, and the social institutions which have grown up, and grown into, our government, both of states and nation. That our national government has made an advance from all European governments, in its social institutions, notwithstanding its sectional and local institution of chattel slavery, no impartial observer can deny; that Europeans, with national or aristocratic pride, have looked, and do look, upon this advance with jealousy and envy, is fully

proven, by teachers and writers from both sides
of the line; that American institutions have enabled
the poorest class of laborers reaching our shores from
Europe to acquire wealth and educate their children,
some of whom have risen to the confidence of the people, and gained the highest honors of the state or nation, has long been known in Europe; and while it has
spurred on the poor to renewed efforts to reach us, it
has brought down the ridicule or contempt of the lineal
descendants of old aristocratic families, who have been
trained to defend the divine right of kings and the kin-
ship of aristocratic families.

But the object of this treatise is to present the true and
real issues between the government of the United States
and most if not all other governments; and also to show
that the same are the issues between the cotton or seceded States in rebellion and the national government;
and that it would be natural to expect foreign governments to sympathize, at least, with the rebels, and, if
they were strong enough, and we weak enough, to also
aid and support them; while, on the other hand, as the
national government would naturally have the sympathy
of the laboring and poorer classes of Europe, they would,
if able and permitted, readily and rapidly move into the
loyal States, and even into their armies, as thousands of
foreigners most nobly and patriotically have done. It
is also intended to show that slavery is only incidental,
and not a fundamental cause of this rebellion, and at
this time proves itself an incubus to the rebels, that
more than any other retards or prevents the expression
of that sympathy which might otherwise be expected
from Europe, as it would bar their country, if successful in gaining a place among the nations, against the

overflowing pauper population of their cities, as they would not labor in competition with those who obtained but a subsistence of rice and rags.   It is also intended to show that *old* governments and systems are doomed to decay, and fail and fall whilst new and more progressive ones are yet to go on and grow; and that to seize a part of ours and set it back under old institutions, would only be to seal its fate for rapid ruin and sure destruction; and that to yield the guardian care of this government over the land, and five or six millions of poor white and free black people in the seceded States, to half a million rebel leaders and their family and chattel appendages, would be a cruel abandonment of dependents and wards, and their landed estates, which of right belong to them; and, further, to show that it is not less cruel, even though these robbed and misguided people are pressed into service, or coaxed and deceived into it against their own interest, and against their best friends, who offered the only hope before them of securing their natural rights.

Three natural human rights, essential and fundamental in all civilized governments, become the basis of the government; and the perpetuity and strength of such governments depend on the location and use of these rights.   If they are secured to all the people, then all the people become proprietors in the government, and will be ever ready, with purse, and hand, and heart, to sustain their government, and will need no gold or other object to stimulate them, — neither Christianity nor the divine right of rulers, not even a national banner, or cross, political or religious glory.   In defending the government, they would only be defending themselves; for the national honor would be their own honor.

It is my purpose to show that these three natural rights have been more generally diffused and maintained among the whole people by the American government than by any other, and extended far more in most of the loyal States than in the rebellious ones; that the cardinal point of issue is the extension of these rights by state and national governments; and that the policy of the cotton States is and has been to restrict and confine these to a small portion of the population; and of the free States, and partially of the border slave States, to extend and secure them to all, or nearly all, of the white population. These three are,

I. THE RIGHT TO LAND.

II. THE RIGHT TO LABOR, AND ITS PRODUCTS.

III. THE RIGHT TO EDUCATION, AND ITS BENEFITS.

## THE RIGHT TO LAND.

THAT every human being is dependent on land for his or her subsistence, is too plain to be argued. That this alone is sufficient to establish the *natural* right of each to a portion of the soil, at least when there is any unoccupied, is as plain as any reasoning or mathematical demonstration can make any claim of nature for her children.

We rigidly maintain, among all civilized nations, the right of each human being to breathe pure air and drink pure water, and never call it stealing in any one to take what he or she wants of either; nor is any one a trespasser who breathes the air pent up in the enclosure of another, nor who drinks the water from another's spring or well. Not less essential is the right of all to the soil; and only the long line of judicial sanctions, starting in robbery, has induced the people to submit to this robbery of a natural right, which they have to purchase back from the descendants of the old robbers.

Blackstone and other eminent writers on the laws of land-titles admit that no title can be sustained if followed back to its source; for it is certain that the maker of the land, who must have been the original owner, neither divided nor transferred the soil to governments nor persons.

Our government sometimes attempts to screen itself under titles received from Indians of large and unsurveyed tracts; but this covering is hardly as good as the fig-leaf garments of the fabled Adam and Eve. The Indians never thought of selling or of owning land, till Europeans came among them; and certainly the chiefs could not have become suddenly heirs to all the land, on the approach of Europeans, by any other right than assumption, which rests on the same authority as the divine right of kings.

How strong is the argument that God, having selected and appointed rulers over the people, gave them also *his* land to sell or distribute? But even admitting (which I am not unwilling to do) that a government has a right to take possession of all unoccupied lands within its limits, and to survey, divide, and limit them to its people, that certainly would not even imply a right to transfer those lands, and thus rob a part or all its inhabitants of their natural rights, more than a right to control the people, or a portion of them, would imply the right to sell them. Natural rights not only inhere *in* persons under governments, but they also adhere *to* persons, and are as inalienable in one case as the other.

A right to life implies a right to the elements on which it depends. The one is inherent, the other adherent; and, as governments pretend to secure the one, they should always secure the other; and, as they do not require a person to purchase life, so they should not require him or her to purchase the elements of life, nor land more than air.

As the earth is the main source of wealth, and also the main source (with its improvements) of taxation, by which governments are carried on and enabled to act, therefore it may be necessary for governments to set up jurisdiction over their respective territories, and survey and divide them, and limit with proper restrictions the occupancy, and secure each against encroachments and trespass. When this is so far secured in a government as to present lands at a very low or merely nominal price, as it has been by our national government, and also by several of the States, graduating and reducing the price, in some instances, to mere cost of survey, it is a nearer approach to securing this natural right to the people than has been secured elsewhere. It is true that England, by our policy, has been compelled to approach it in her colonies; but it is directly opposed to her home system, and incorporated in the very existence of ours.

The people of the Northern States have long since seen and demanded their right to a share of the government lands, in homestead grants, and would long since have secured it, through Congress, but for the opposition of the cotton States, whose opposition originated in their social system, which has ever been opposed to the division of lands into small estates and homesteads for all the people. Some of their politicians have, it is true, at times, seemed to favor this measure for political purposes, but were always careful to have it defeated at the end, as they always did measures which carried forward the distinctive policy of the North, that conflicted with their own.

In the early settlement of the colonies that compose the United States, the land was mostly granted in large tracts to individuals or companies, by powers who, of course, had no title to convey, whether English, French, Spanish, or Indian. In that portion now in rebellion these grants were divided, it is true, but still retained in large family estates, as they must necessarily be for the cultivation successfully of cotton, sugar, rice, and tobacco, by slave labor. As this slave labor produced in abundance not only the comforts and luxuries of life, but great wealth also for many families, the owners were not under a necessity of selling or subdividing, except to heirs, and, in most of these cases, one could easily buy out the other, who would choose to travel or trade on abundant means; and, as the climate and soil were such that the poor could subsist almost without labor, and the planters had adopted a system of letting the poor whites live (or stay) on their lands, as tenants at will, without rent; and as the tendency of ignorance and poverty, aided by the effect of that climate, led the landless whites into the most stupid indolence, and thus separated them, socially, widely from the proud and haughty planters; and as the planters only were represented in the government, both state and national, they, of course, would rigidly adhere to the system and its distinctions, including the monop-

oly of the soil, which they have done, till this has become
one of the principal causes and issues of this rebellion.

On the other hand, the large grants in New England and the Northern States, mostly rough, rocky,
mountains, and often almost worthless to the owners,
and never adapted to slave labor, and which when new
would not, for many years, pay for wages-labor, were
readily and gladly divided and subdivided, and sold to
actual settlers; so that, often, a man could buy a farm
(or land to make one) for a mug of flip, or, often, a
very good tract for one year's work, or a small share of
the first ten years' crops. This system resulted in making nearly every family in many towns freeholders, and,
of course, voters (or a part of each family), secured
their interest in the government and its institutions,
and soon left only a small sediment of landless poor,
who were usually either females or worthless males,
who, with the increased stimulus of securing themselves
from that northern climate, and the imperative demand
of the long winters for warm clothes, good fuel, and
plenty of food, were still too indolent to get homes and
soil for almost nothing, The females were of course
excused for being landless, as they are taught in
all Christian countries to get husbands, and depend on
them for homes. So strong has been the sentiment,
obtained in New England, New York, and Pennsylvania, and carried westward with their emigrants to the
new States and broad prairies, that they have, in many
townships and villages, attempted, often successfully, to
force the larger landholders to sell or divide, by taxing
them exorbitantly; and most of the speculators have
been compelled to yield, or fail and have their lands
sold by creditors, or for taxes.

Any government which, either by its laws or its social system, divides its lands among nearly all its inhabitants, making all or nearly all families freeholders, and sustains itself by taxes collected on the improvements and wealth, without taxing the enterprise or energy, has laid in the most durable cement the chief corner-stone of its perpetuity, and one on which it can build with the best of security for strength and durability. Our national government has done much in this direction, and the free States much, also. And any government that robs a large portion of its inhabitants of this right to the soil, either by keeping the prices too high, or by a social system they cannot change, and thus monopolizes the soil in possession of a few families, has laid the foundation for revolution and ultimate ruin.

European nations have done much in this way, and the cotton (or seceded) States of the United States have done even more than France, little less than England at home, and far more than England in her colonies. A landed aristocracy of planters, many of whom sprang originally from the dregs of society in Europe, hold complete sway over the rebellion, and attempt to force the thousands of landless poor to fight and endure all sorts of privations and hardships, to sustain them in the monopoly, and, if successful, will continue to rob and oppress them, and make from them the soldiers of a standing army, to assist in robbing their children of their natural rights, and monopolizing the land and all that is valuable in social life.

A nation rooted in the soil by the freehold of most of its inhabitants, and with their right secured by law against every species of robbery that could monopolize it and pauper them by placing it beyond their reach, would, in time of war, need no conscriptions or drafting. Every man able to bear arms, if needed, would rush to the defence of his country; for his country would be his home, and a home worth defending. This is one of the reasons that in the present struggle the loyal States have so readily and patriotically raised an immense army without the application of force, which in some way was almost immediately resorted to by the rebels to bring their landless and ignorant poor into the ranks, and to keep them there without pay of any value.

When the loyal States shall have settled this rebellion, and firmly established the democratic policy of the North, including this right to soil, the large amount of lands, in the old estates, that will be brought into market, added to the vast amount of public lands still unsold, and the large tracts of new land held loosely by the speculators, will for many years keep the price within the reach of all industrious persons, even females; and, during this period, the rapidly spreading principles of land-reform will secure land limitation, and thus root and anchor the entire free population in the soil, and make a nation of freeholders, which will also, ultimately, secure most of the dwellings and gardens in title to the females, and the agricultural and other lands, mills, shops, etc., to the male portion.

Thus we move, first to secure the rights of all *men*, and then of the women. Man, having assumed the right to make and control all laws relating to land and to woman, will, of course, first secure his own interest, as he discovers it, and then that of the other sex, over which he assumes guardianship.

There is surely a brighter day dawning for the land-less, when this crisis is over, and democracy has triumphed over aristocracy, as it certainly must.

---

## THE RIGHT TO LABOR.

THE second essential and inalienable right of all men and all women is the right to labor and its products; and any system of government or society which deprives any considerable number of the people of this right, is ruinous, not only to that part of the community, but to the whole organization, which must thereby be sooner or later overthrown. In the result, it will not make much difference whether they be deprived or prevented by law directly, or by fashion and pride, prejudice and contempt, or by the monopoly of capital and land so as to prevent them the means of labor.

That system which has been practised in the cotton States, since the settlement of them, of purchasing and holding a portion of the race, and forcing the labor from them, by degrading both them and the labor, almost entirely excludes it from the other part of society; and, although it may enrich a few, and impoverish many, it must be ruinous to the whole, — first, and most rapidly, to those who are deprived of it and its products, by reducing, as it has in the Sandhillers and other poor whites, one part below the chaftel laborers, and driving another part into idleness, wealth, luxury, and lust, to physical weakness and rapid and sure destruction.

This is and has been the effect in those sections

where labor has been confined almost exclusively to slaves, and less so in the border slave States, where it has been slightly mixed with white or free labor.

In the first settlement of New England, the severity of climate and sterility of soil required all able hands to labor to secure the necessaries of life. Once started in general industry, they made it not only respectable but honorable, and continued it so, even when it was not required to procure necessaries, till it brought comforts also; and, still maintaining its credit and standing, with and by it they have drawn from it and their sterile soil very many luxuries, even, and surrounded their homes and hills with more social and domestic comforts to the whole population than can be found in any section of the world, except, perhaps, some small sections with better soil and climate, and settled by emigrants from their homes, and carrying their system and industry with them.

New England, New York, New Jersey and Pennsylvania, incorporated labor into their social system, making it respectable and partially honorable, and carrying it westward and northward, with their emigrants, into all new settlements, around the lakes, and over the Alleghanies, the Ohio, and upper Mississippi, to the foot of the Rocky Mountains, and also around the water-path to the Pacific coast, and settling and controlling California and Oregon. This rapid spread of the social system of these States, with labor foremost and uppermost, greatly aided by the large amount of immigrant laborers from Europe, had, by its natural superiority, rapidly outrun the opposite system of the cotton States, with its chattel laborers and degraded industry, although they had many advantages of soil and climate, with

2*

plenty of uncultivated lands at home, and new lands at the westward.

Thus the monopoly of the soil and labor, and consequent degradation of the latter, belonged to the social system of the cotton States; and the partial freedom of both, with the respectability of labor, belonged to the North. Of course these advantages of themselves would be sufficient to bring them the laboring European emigrants, which, added to their own advantages, would enable them to rapidly outrun their competitors, as they have done, in settling new districts.

But this is only a description of the two extremes, or the leading systems, so opposite, and yet incorporated under the same government, and contending for the mastery. There was and is, also, a "middle ground," which will be described in these pages, with its important part especially, in the rebellion.

Let us turn to the _physiological_ law of labor, which was _not_ set upon man as a curse,—as related in the old Jewish fable, and carried out in our system of chattel slavery and the prison discipline of the States,—but which was entailed by mother Nature on us as a rich inheritance, if properly used, and set as a blessing in the system of human growth and development, like fire and water, useful to all, if properly exercised, and destructive as they are at some times and places. Water quenches thirst and cleanses us, but may also drown us. Fire warms us and cooks our dinner, but may burn our hands or bodies also. So of labor; the best of blessings to all, but should be regulated by reason, use, and laws of health.

Nature has dropped a curse on those who will not labor, by which they are physically blighted, and soon

become incompetent to give existence to offspring with
sufficient vital force to develop a muscular system and
keep up the original stock. Thus, under the monopolizing system of the cotton States, the planters and
loafers become slender, and soon dwarf in muscle and
form, while the laborers become muscular and athletic;
and in a few generations the intellect will follow, and
then those once at the top go to the bottom, and the
bottom goes to the top, and society is overturned. This
is the natural tendency in the cotton States, with their
monopolies of land in one class and labor in another.

The planters can hardly have been blind to this fact,
with the statistics before them of the rapid increase of
slaves, both in numbers and muscular force, and the
weakening muscular power of the whites, with its nerv-
ous and fractious irritability, which has been so promi-
nent, in and out of Congress, for the last quarter of a
century, and which has at last wrought itself up to the
pitch of a fighting rebellion; while their leading city of
Charleston, S. C., shows, by the returns of the census,
that it had decreased in population three thousand
between 1850 and 1860; while even the increase of
slaves and slave-labor has not been able to keep their
section of the country up (with all its advantages of
soil and climate) to the northern portion, in wealth, influence, enterprise, population, or representation; and
hence its factious leaders get mad, and prove true the
sentiment of the wag of the *Atlantic Monthly*:

> "Plain proof her cause an't strong, —
> The one that fust gits mad 's most ollers wrong."

If the earnings of the laborers of the cotton States,

or those of England, were secured to themselves, they would soon own the whole property, real and personal; but in the South the arbitrary system of ownership of the laborers of course robs them, and in England the arbitrary system of monopoly and taxation is nearly as oppressive, taking seventy-five per cent. of their earnings, and leaving the balance, which is hardly sufficient for subsistence; thus keeping them in a complete state of submission and subjection, discipline and obedience. Rob them first, and then give them a pittance of their own earnings to subsist on, and thus gain the credit of charity and goodness, and the love and devotion of the people to the government, is the system and policy of England. But the South has not gained the love and devotion of her slaves; for she degrades and sells them, as cattle and horses, in addition to robbing them of their earnings.

Slavery is sometimes defended as a charitable institution of apprenticeship; but, if it is so, it is strange that the owners are so rapidly enriching themselves out of it, and keeping the objects as poor and ignorant as at first, except in so far as the labor itself develops them. Apprentices are usually taught something, and set free with it. If slavery is a charitable system, it is certainly the only one I have ever heard of that rapidly enriches those who contribute, and explains why so many mercenary and selfish persons engage in it, as they get gain and credit for charity at the same time, and by the same acts.

Those who put forward slavery as the only or main cause of the present rebellion, are greatly mistaken. The cause lies deeper, and is broader, but takes in slavery as one of the principal ingredients in the "charmed pot" of secession and rebellion, though an ingredient that would surely, in time, overturn the new government, by a power and a right superior to either one in the present combined attempt to set up a new national government.

Any government which secures to all its people labor, and makes it respectable and honorable, and secures to the laborers their earnings, will root itself in the hearts and homes of the people, and bind them to its defence and support; and they will come without compulsion to its defence, with their full pockets, hard hands, and warm hearts, as is illustrated by the rush of volunteers into the service of the government, from the loyal States, to put down the present rebellion. And although the free States have not fully secured to each the rights of all people to land and labor, and the products of both, yet they have come so much nearer to it than the South, or any conspicuous government in Europe, that they are in advance in securing human rights, and of course should be in patriotism and loyalty, which they are now proving to be so.

Labor is the source of all wealth that is legitimately wealth. All else is plunder. Past labor is capital, and may be made to reproduce itself, if in productive machinery, stock, fruit-trees, land-improvements, or boats, railroads, etc.; but money, which is used only for a currency, is non-productive property, and *never* is entitled to interest or usury. All laws establishing or regulating interest should be at once repealed, and let currency first regulate its own value and sale; and, after a few years, the common sense of the people would reduce usury to a mere nominal rate, or nothing. It is the constant tampering of law-makers with currency that keeps

up the excitement and speculation which are ever robbing the poor laborer for the increasing accumulations
of the rich.

When I was a member of the State Senate of Wisconsin, by great exertion I secured the repeal of the usury
laws of that State, and in two years the people were
beginning to feel the benefits, when the renewed efforts
of bankers, brokers, and money-shavers secured the re-
enactment of a system of usury, in time to check the
growing knowledge of the people, which in a few more
years would have prevented them forever.

As soon as the people can feel and understand their
rights and interests, in the free States, they will secure
and hold them; but all systems of tyranny, oppression,
and robbery, are perpetuated by and through the ignorance of the victims. Were the English laborers made
fully acquainted with the fact that they are the source
of the wealth of England, which is ever taken from
them, and placed beyond their reach by a few capital-
ists who control the government and religion, they
could not long be made to submit to it. In truth, the
wealth of England belongs to her poor operatives.
They have developed the resources of her mines, and
wrought the raw material into her fine and high-priced
fabrics. Why should they not have her wealth, and
enjoy her treasures?

There is a gulf almost as wide, between the poor
laborers of England and her aristocracy, as between the
planters and slaves of the cotton States. The aristocracy cannot sell the operatives, but they *can* starve
them. The planters can sell the slaves, but they *cannot*
starve them; for their law and public opinion will interfere, as potently as the law and opinion of England

against selling. The planter can whip with a lash of small cords; the aristocrat can whip with the starving mouths of small children crying to parents for bread. One parts husband and wife by sale; the other by hunger and death. Both harp and carp about charity, and talk the religion of Jesus, who only knew and loved the poor, and condemned the rich more severely than any treatise of mine can. He is said to have overturned with his own hands the tables of the money-changers; yet here are the money-changers lauding his name, and robbing still, with a tighter hand than ancient Jew or Egyptian. Only the United States government and the loyal States have made some sure steps of approach to a natural system of human rights, and alarmed the tyrants of Europe and the aristocratic slaveholding planters of this country. We have sung the songs of labor; we have honored the workman, and branded with honor the hard hand of toil; and for it we meet the contempt of the aristocracy of all countries, even our own where we are weak, and their hatred where we are strong; hence the bitter and vindictive spirit that manifests itself among the chivalry in rebellion and their sympathizing friends. No terms of contempt in our language are equal to the desire of expressing their feelings, and they rake the dregs of all languages, and even coin words, for bombastic utterances of southern chivalry. It is the natural expression of an aristocratic contempt for labor and laborers, and is spit out of the mouth of chivalry upon the whole people of the North, who protect, and defend, and perform labor; hence they are the "mud-sills" and operatives of the nation; but if we pull out the mud-sills, the mill will be likely to fall and wash away in the first freshet.

Having travelled extensively, for over ten years, and become thoroughly acquainted with the social condition of society East, West, and North, and, by adding testimony to observation, also with the South, I am enabled to state positively that the laboring men and women are the superior class of society. They are more moral, more honest, more truly religious, more virtuous, more charitable, etc. They are less dissipated, less licentious, less bigoted, less proud, less given to gambling, stealing, lying, cheating, deceiving, and robbing each other; in fact, they are the bone and sinew of the nation; and if it continues in prosperity, it must be by protecting this class, and securing to them their earnings and natural rights, and preparing them to take part in all the business affairs of the country.

If there is truth in the old maxim, "*Labor omnia vincit,*" certainly the laborers must some day conquer aristocracy, and the slaves must rise to the surface of society, and conquer their oppressors. So, also, must the operatives of England, as, in fact, the laborers of New England already have; and hence the advanced condition and government of the free States, by and under which the people have grown into a better condition than in any other country.

It is plain to any student of nature and physiology that, in three or four generations, if immigration were prevented, the slaves would overthrow their masters' power, and take the government into their own hands, at the cost of life and treasure to the masters; and certainly no power could justly interfere which had recognized the right in the present rebellion of the seceded States to overturn their government, and set up a new one on its ruins. Certainly a rebellion of the oppressed laborers, who had earned the wealth of the country, and an attempt to take it and control it, and gain their freedom, could not be called a wicked or unjust one.

"Tickets buying, taking, selling, but into the feast never once going ,
Many sweating, ploughing, thrashing, and then the chaff for payment
    receiving ;
A few idly owning, and they the wheat continually claiming."
                                                    LEAVES OF GRASS.

Truly said, as many things are in the same book, by that most radical and reckless American author, **Walt Whitman.**

---

## THE RIGHT TO EDUCATION.

DURING the last quarter of a century, many able writers have been quite successful in proving that all children have a natural right to education ; at least, sufficient to hold intellectual correspondence with other minds, present and absent. Our national government has recognized this right partially, in granting large tracts of land to new States, to found schools free to all children ; and the governments of the free States have recognized it still more fully, in opening schools free to all children, and supporting them by taxation on the property in the several districts.

Several of the new States have, by the aid of the lands, opened, not only common schools, but academies, and even colleges, free to all ; thus carrying forward the early habits and teachings of New England, and New York, and Pennsylvania.

Few persons can be found, in New England, between

3

the ages of fifteen and twenty-five years, who cannot read; and still less, in proportion, will be found, who were born in some of the Western States where the townships are settled as thoroughly as in New England. But an entirely different system prevails in the cotton States. The wealthy families of planters educate finely and thoroughly their children, but make no provision for the poor, and never think of acknowledging it as the *right* of their children, — a right really as sacred as the right to life and liberty. They build no school-houses for poor children, either white or black, and even prohibit by law the education of their laboring blacks, who earn nearly all their wealth. Of course such an unjust system of robbery cannot prosper long, if there is justice in God's government. But the robbery of the poor whites is nearly as great and cruel; for they not only rob them of land and education, but of labor also, which they leave to the blacks; and it *is* a blessing to them, even if it be forced, and sometimes extravagantly hard.

It would be more difficult, in the cotton States, to find a poor white person, between the ages referred to, who could read, than to find one in New England who could not.

Thus poverty, ignorance, and idleness, separate the rich and poor in the South, but not in the North; and hence the wide difference in the social systems of the cotton and corn States.

In the first settlement of New England and New York the people were brought upon an equality by the common necessity for labor; and soon followed the almost common freehold of families, and also the common and united effort to have schools for all the children. Not even the few blacks were excluded; for they were recognized as of a common humanity, and as having a common necessity for land, labor, and education.

The commencement of general education in New England was a religious movement of the Puritans, who contended for the right and *necessity* of having all people read the Bible; much of their zeal arising from the bitter and persistent opposition to the Catholics, who did not deem it necessary, if convenient, for Christians to read that Holy Book. But the Puritans thought all should read God's word; and thus, with the expectation of far different results, they began that system of general education which has already nearly swamped the Bible, and turned its wonderful mysteries into fables, and loosened and dissipated, instead of tightening and establishing the religion of the fathers. But other great and good results followed.

These three great and all-important° rights were, and are, and ever have been, more generally distributed and secured to the whole people, by New England and her descendants, than by any government or country; and New York, and Pennsylvania, and New Jersey, of the old States, followed closely after; and the descendants of these States have ever and successfully carried forward these rights, as they settled more western States and territories.

These wide distinctions form the basis of antagonism, and the cause of the present rebellion, in which slavery is only an ingredient, but a very irritating one, and one on which the South could get up more prejudice and hatred than on any other; and hence it has been used as the cause, partly by both North and South.

Had the cotton States stated the true ground of

the rebellion and cause of secession and resistance to the government, few of the poor whites would have been found in the ranks of their armies, if, indeed, an army could have been raised, which is doubtful. The political leaders, knowing this, resorted to deception, and once more imposed upon the poor whites, who had already been robbed of the three great natural rights, and, working up in them a bitter prejudice against abolitionists, who had often been very injudicious in their attacks on slavery and slave-holders, made the ignorant believe the government was in the hands of abolitionists, and that all the bitterness of some fiery and vindictive haters of all who lived in a land of slavery was to be visited upon the whole South. The planters and most of the leaders knew better, but the poor people did not, and thus were drawn into armies, to fight against their own rights and interests, and the only hope before them of securing for their children their natural rights to land, labor, and education, of which the social system of the South has, and, if it can perpetuate itself, ever will rob them.

The true and real issue of the rebellion is democracy or aristocracy, — monopoly or equality. Which shall control the nation has been settled by the success of the northern system in the new states and territories, and by the settled policy of the government.

The contest over the admission of Missouri ended in ceding it to the slave system; but the settlement of northerners, and the northern enterprise that controlled its great commercial city, soon gave its policy, system, and influence to the other side; while Arkansas, which was given up to aristocracy, to slavery and alligators, has remained almost a country of barbarians; and Mich·

igan, with the opposite policy, and in a more severe climate, and with far more sterile soil, has a population which, for intelligence and enterprise, cannot be excelled in the West, and which, with her free academies and college, places her near the head of the States; while Arkansas and Florida contend for the foot, although entering the Union about the same time, with equal advantages, except the false social system. Labor and education are almost universal in Michigan, and poverty and ignorance in Arkansas, with a few rich planters scattered over the State.

3*

# BORDER STATES.

## NOW OR NEVER.

"Listen, young heroes! your country is calling!
    Time strikes the hour for the brave and the true
Now, while the foremost are fighting and falling,
    Fill up the ranks they have opened for you!

"You, whom the fathers made free and defended,
    Stain not the scroll that emblazons their fame
You, whose fair heritage spotless descended,
    Leave not your children a birthright of shame!

"Stay not for questions, while Freedom stands gasping .
    Wait not till Honor lies wrapped in his pall!
Brief the lips' meeting be, swift the hands' clasping, —
    ' Off for the wars' is enough for them all!

"Break from the arms that would fondly caress you!
    Hark! 'tis the bugle-blast, sabres are drawn!
Mothers shall pray for you, fathers shall bless you,
    Maidens shall weep for you when you are gone!

"Never or now! cries the blood of a nation,
    Poured on the turf where the red rose should bloom ;
Now is the day and the hour of salvation ;
    Never or now! peals the trumpet of doom!

"Never or now! roars the hoarse-throated cannon,
    Through the black canopy blotting the skies ;
Never or now! flaps the shell-blasted pennon
    O'er the deep ooze where the Cumberland lies

"From the foul dens where our brothers are dying,
    Aliens and foes in the land of their birth,

(80)

From the rank swamps where our martyrs are lying,
Pleading in vain for a handful of earth ;

" From the hot plains where they perish outnumbered,
Furrowed and ridged with the battle-field's plough,
Comes the loud summons ; too long you have slumbered ;
Here the last angel-trump — Never or Now ! "

THERE are no border free States. Their policy is uniform on these subjects, and their social system the same, except a slight variation in the section of Ohio, Indiana and Illinois, along the Ohio river, among a population made up mostly of immigrants from slave States; and, in this section, the variation is mainly in education, they having followed the North in the system of labor and land, and the South in that of education. But they have, of late, been much changed toward the northern system of schools also.

But in Delaware and Maryland, Virginia and Kentucky, the systems of slavery and aristocracy have been drying up, and free white, or wages labor, taking their places. Old plantations have been divided or sold to Yankees, and school-houses have sprung up along the northern border of those States; and, so far as the northern social system has prevailed, loyal sentiment and a devotion to the government have gone with it.

It is curious to note the persons who were rebellious, or sympathized with the rebels, in these States. They were composed of two classes, the few rich landholders and aristocrats, and the miserable poor rabble who had no land or education, and were pressed from labor by slavery. The latter were the supple tools of the first, and ready to enter ignorantly into any scheme for breaking up the government, to which they charged their wrongs, which were really chargeable to the very aristocrats who were leading them to ruin, and on false issues entirely.

The issues of this contest or trial of democracy, are *in* the border slave States, and *between* the cotton and northern States; hence the division in those States, and the untiring efforts of a few wealthy and many poor and ignorant to carry these States with the cotton States, that they might thereby continue and perpetuate their conditions and distinctions of society.

It is a curious principle in society that the "upper ten and lower million" each is attached to and tries to perpetuate its conditions, as much as the middle classes. Both of these, in which society switches out, had their affinities in the South, and they came near carrying Baltimore and Washington, as they did Richmond, Memphis, and Nashville. They tried, also, but were too weak, in St. Louis and Louisville, and in Wheeling weaker still.

The leaders in the rebellion had long been planning for the outbreak, and had secured the election of governors in Missouri, Kentucky, Virginia and Tennessee, from their own ranks, and the legislatures of Missouri and Maryland, but had been defeated in securing the governor in Maryland; and the legislatures of Kentucky and Virginia were, at best, doubtful. But in all these States the middle classes were loyal; the laboring freeholders, and most of the laborers of all classes, were loyal and true to the old government and banner; but the rabble, led and urged on by the few wealthy aristocrats, with most of the offices in their hands, soon overpowered them in Eastern Virginia, in Tennessee, and small sections of Kentucky and Maryland; but in all the districts where the rebels prevailed it was where the

southern society prevailed, with a few wealthy aristocrats for leaders, and an ignorant, lazy and poor rabble
for followers.

Baltimore had, for several years, shown the prevalence
of this latter class, in her mobs and riots, which had
been nearly suppressed for a year previous to the general outbreak. The firmness of Gov. Hicks, supported
by the slow but sure democracy or middle classes of his
State, saved Maryland from ruin and general bankruptcy.
The large preponderance of this class over both the
others, in Western Virginia, saved that section of the
Old Dominion; while the preponderance of the other
two classes in Eastern Virginia carried it to the rebels, with the officers who had been selected and elected
for the very purpose by impositions upon the honest
and industrious voters.

It is well known that neither Letcher, in Virginia,
nor Magoffin, in Kentucky, nor Jackson, in Missouri,
could have been elected, nor even Harris, in Tennessee,
had the issue of a dissolution of the Union or secession been before the people when they were chosen;
for a majority of the voters in all those States, if not in
the others, have ever been loyal to the old government.
In Delaware, slavery and aristocracy were so nearly
dried up that two or three leading aristocrats had little
influence in leading her out of the national constella-
tion.

The whole issue was a hard but fair trial of democracy in the border slave States. The more they had
been depleted of slavery, and the more they had suffered by loss of slaves, the more had free. labor, small
farms and schools, crept in among them, and, consequently, democracy and human rights, and hence, con-

sequently, a devotion to the Union; while the leaders were trying to make the ignorant whites in the cotton States believe one of the great causes of complaint was that fugitives could not be caught and returned. Yet here was the lie, in the fact that the most depleted districts of the slave States were the most loyal; and South Carolina and Florida, which had lost no fugitives worth naming, were the most united and first in the rebellion; because there was the most complete society of inclusive and exclusive monopoly and robbery.

It was evident, from the first, that the leaders in the rebellion had not designed to retain in the new confederacy the border slave States, not even Virginia or Kentucky; but, as these were rich States, they designed to seize and carry off all they could, both of men and property; hence the hasty removal of their congress and main army into Eastern Virginia, the richest section in the rebel jurisdiction, yet one they had not expected to hold, but knew they could devour. They started with the declaration that cotton was king; but cotton was never king in Virginia, or Maryland, or Kentucky, — not even in North Carolina or Tennessee; but the latter were required for a border to the kingdom of cotton, and to give a nearly straight line across the country, leaving all north of North Carolina, Tennessee, and Arkansas; and, as they intended to hold portions of territory north of this line till the final settlement, they could cede it in exchange for Fort Pickens, and other points, on the the east or west, which might be in possession of the Union. Then cotton would surely be king, and sugar queen, and slave labor profitable, which it never was in the corn and stock growing districts.

'Could the new government have taken in all the slave States, the same issues, in part, and difference of society would exist that did before, and would, in time, divide again; or the free labor would, if too weak to contend for itself, soon join with the slaves, and lead in a rebellion, and overthrow the new government; but could they divide on the north line of North Carolina, Tennessee and Arkansas, they would only have a feeble border of free labor, and, with the vast superiority of slaveholders and slave labor, would be able to hold out a long time against the influence of democracy; and they would also, by this line, leave a wide border on the side of the Union, which would require a long time to be brought in fully to the acceptance and development of the northern sentiment and system; whilst, on the other hand, if they took in all the slave States, they would be joined closely to the very system that had crowded them into the present rebellion.

While the honest and industrious loyal people of the border slave States were carrying on their farms, unsuspecting and confident, the scheming demagogues and reckless politicians were planning their ruin, and the overthrow of the government under which they had gained all they had of liberty, and all the security they held for their rights.

A majority of the people in Virginia, North Carolina, Kentucky, Tennessee, and probably in Georgia and Texas, were prepared for a system of democracy and free labor, and would soon secure general and free education; after which they would be secure against aristocracy, and rebellion of tyrants and land lords, or cotton and slave lords.

Could the whole people of the border slave States

have been awakened to their true interest and the true
issues of the rebellion, they would have put it down,
not only in their own borders, but over the whole rebellious region, for they had the power, by their connec-
tion and sympathy with the poor people of the South,
before the rebels had aroused a prejudice among
the ignorant against the people of the northern slave
States. They could therefore have settled at once the
whole difficulty by representing the true issue to them.
But the leaders had taken pains to keep the faces and
prejudices turned to the North, and set against their
true friends, or to keep them divided and confused
among themselves. They were not able to do this
effectually in Missouri, in Kentucky, in Maryland, nor in
Western Virginia; but in Eastern Virginia, Tennessee,
North Carolina, Arkansas, and parts of Missouri, they
did fully succeed, and made some robberies in other
parts, where they could not create a general confusion.
It was also plain that they did not intend or expect to
retain the border slave States; for they made extraor-
dinary efforts to destroy property, both public and
private, and to devastate the region, leaving as little
trace of civilization as possible.

The attempt to get possession of Louisville, the great
commercial city of Kentucky, was, of course, unsuccess-
ful, because it was too near Indiana and Ohio, and too
strongly impregnated with northern principles and sen-
timents. But had it been as near the cotton region as
Nashville, it could have been as easily carried by a
southern military force, while, like the latter, it would
have contained as loyal people as before the rebellion
began. Louisville represents and nearly controls Kentucky, as St. Louis does Missouri. Could the rebels

have seized these large cities, they would have controlled the States through them, as they did Virginia through Richmond, and Tennessee by Nashville and Memphis, and both of them against the voice of the people of the States.

These divided States have been the districts of terrible devastation and horrible crimes, many of which will never be written. It has been to them the trial of democracy; and its complete victory will come to them with the suppression of the rebellion, after which they will rapidly rise from the sources of ruin, and, invigorated by a large northern immigration, they will soon present the freeholders and laborers and school-houses of the more northern States, and their immense hidden resources will then be developed, as they never could be by the slave system, nor by the half-and-half system and stupid indolence that have been so prevalent for many years, caused by the decay of the old plantation system of partial aristocracy.

Arkansas was and is little else than an appendage to Memphis, Tennessee. That city would carry it in or out of the Union, as it was mainly dependent on it for all it bought or sold, or knew of the world.

Texas was a land of chivalry, and had many brave men, who were fond of fight, and cared little whom they fought, or what they fought for. They would fight as well in rebellion as for the government against Mexico. They were and are the best soldiers in the southern army, and the most reckless and wicked when loose in cities or country. It is doubtful whether she is a loyal State, or not, as much depends on these circumstances; but her men are brave and reckless.

In speaking of democracy I have no allusion to the

4

political parties of the nation; for the Secession and
Abolition, Whig and Democrat, Republican and Free-
soil, have each advocated and opposed, more or less,
some democratic principles. For instance, no party,
except the seceding aristocracy, has more strenuously
opposed the democratic principle of woman's equal
right to vote, than the national democracy. While they
have contended for the right of all, who are subject to
laws and taxes, to participate in making the laws, yet,
though women and even negroes were subject to laws
and taxes equally with males and whites, still they
would not let them participate. Neither would any
other party. Even the abolitionists, who would allow
negroes their rights, would exclude and deprive their
own wives and daughters, who had as many natural
rights as themselves which should be secured by statute laws, under democratic principles. When all are
equally educated these rights will be secured to them.
Then will another democratic principle triumph in our
country, making brighter its historic pages.

But this principle of equal or universal suffrage is of
less importance than the three fundamental ones which
form the basis of our government, and the gist of this
treatise. No country can prosper long, and no government be permanent, unless these three are secured to
the people, but may without others of less vital importance.

It would be an interesting history that should record
the spread, growth and progress of true democracy in
the northern slave States: the slow division of large
plantations and land grants in many neighborhoods;
the steady increase of free and hand labor of white men
and women, and the steady decrease of slaves and their

value for service at home; the slow growth and spread
of the schools, and gradual extension of education to
the girls and the poor white children,—all mainly from
more northern influence, and immigration from the free
States. Old Virginia has realized this change on her
"tired lands" more than many districts of the South,
and slavery has ceased to be profitable (if it ever was
so), except in the raising of slaves for market; and this
is true of Kentucky and most of Tennessee.

It was evident, from the commencement of action
among the rebels, that they did not intend to have the
cotton States injured by the war more than possible,
but to let it expose, devastate and destroy the border States. They had not power to reach and devastate a free State; but, by drawing out all they could
from Maryland, Kentucky, Missouri, etc., to put them
into the most exposed positions, and move the troops
from farther South into Virginia, Kentucky and Tennessee, and thus to feed upon those States where there
were plenty of loyal people to plunder and press into
service. The official list—if we could ever get one—
of the rebels killed, would show this policy, and that
they exposed most the volunteers from States they did
not want or expect to hold; whilst South Carolina, which
inaugurated the movement, kept out of danger mostly,
and only put her troops forward in a contest like that
of taking Sumter, in its defenceless condition, which
they could never have taken had the little State of
Rhode Island alone been permitted to defend it and
secure it before attacked.

The best soldiers in the rebel army were those
drawn from the border States, and they had the brunt
of the contest. The chivalry was of little account,

except for bombastic words, single-handed duels, and guerilla bands; and when the border States are broken and restored to loyalty, all that will be left of that army will be guerilla bands of rebel plunderers.

Such is the character of that aristocratic monopoly which has been the ruin of the South, and from which this revolution will partially restore them — the border States first, and the cotton States last.

While the rebels have crowded the border State troops into the most dangerous positions (perhaps partly because they are the bravest), and have endeavored to devastate and destroy, and carry off negroes and property, on the other hand the national army has protected families and men, property and even slaves, and hardly invited from them volunteers; but the soldiers from Ohio and Indiana mainly drove the rebels from even Western Virginia; and those from Ohio, Indiana and Illinois, did most of the fighting in Kentucky and Tennessee; and the Illinois, Iowa, Kansas and Minnesota troops were side by side with the true men of Missouri in her delivery from the rebel rule. It is true the Kentucky, Tennessee, Virginia and Maryland soldiers were good and brave, and did good service when in action; but they were seldom pressed or pressing forward to the rescue even of their own rebellious territory, in the earlier part of the war. It was found that Wisconsin, Michigan, Indiana and New York soldiers were better guards of Baltimore than the regiments of their own State — not because more loyal, but because composed of steadier men, and better subjects to order, decency and law, easier disciplined and educated. This was the effect of democracy, or the principles I have laid down in this treatise.

As fast as the government arms were successful, public and private property was protected; as far and fast as the rebels progressed north in the border States, both were used, and if they retreated it was usually destroyed, as in their attempts to destroy Baltimore, first, by cutting it off from the east, west and north by railroad, and forcing it into the hands of a mob, by which it would have been declared a rebel city, with no chance of escape from destruction from the army of the Union at the first attack. Their wanton destruction of the Baltimore and Ohio Railroad will long be remembered against them by Baltimorians, as this was its main artery of trade; but the Union forces protected it, and its repair soon as practicable. And the same is true of all other roads and avenues of trade, except the stone blockade of Charleston, S. C., which could *not* be justified either by our policy or any necessity, and which the sober judgment of the world and the historian will condemn as contrary to the best policy of the government, and a mistake for which no excuse will be found in the sober second thought of the people.

As the border slave States have been the greatest sufferers in the rebellion, so they will feel first and most the benefits. Slavery will soon disappear from them, and free labor and schools will spring up in them rapidly after the restoration of peace, and a new policy and new men will come to the surface and take the lead, the middle classes letting down the aristocracy to their level; for where confiscation or sacrifice to the rebellion does not waste or reduce the large estates, the taxes to pay for the war will do it; for the property in the nation must pay the bills; and the men, and mostly the moderately poor men, must do the work and fighting.

4*

and get the pay. This will greatly reduce our aristocracy of wealth in all parts of the country, but most in
the border slave States of any part of the loyal, and
must nearly destroy it also in the cotton States. This
will be a national blessing arising from the war.

## SLAVERY.

THAT slavery has had a conspicuous part in the present rebellion, no one denies. That it is an essential
ingredient in southern society, is equally undeniable.
That it is a barrier to democracy, which must be removed by the success of the latter, cannot be seriously
questioned. That it is an evil, if not a blighting curse,
to any country, no disinterested, candid and unprej-
udiced individual will deny. But that it has been
the sole, or principal, cause of the great rebellion of
1861 and '62, as thousands honestly believe, is not sustained by an examination of the subject. It is plain
that it has only been used as the best subject on which
to arouse a public prejudice in both sections of the
country, but mainly by the southern leaders to gain a
unanimity of sentiment and coöperation of the poor
whites in the rebellion of the aristocrats; and it has
entered so essentially into the politics of the North,
that many see no other issue.

I shall present here a part of the evidences in support of my position, and leave the subject for reflection

with the reader, sure that time will show the correctness of my reasoning.

1. The section of country which had suffered most
by loss and depreciation of slave property, and of plantations cultivated by slaves, was last and least in the
rebellion, and much of it could not be drawn or driven
into conflict with the national government, for reasons
which I have elsewhere stated; when, if the defence
of slavery had been the cause, these should have taken
the lead.

2. The States which took the lead, and were most
united in the rebellion, were those that had suffered
least, or not at all, in the depreciation of slave property
and slave labor and large plantations, for reasons elsewhere given, and which were far more connected with
aristocracy and monopoly than with slavery. The cotton and cane States took the lead in the rebellion, not
because slavery was profitable there, and only there,
but because aristocracy and monopoly were most complete there, and democracy had not yet gained a foot-
hold in sufficient force to contend with them.

3. The first attempt to set up a new nation, and establish an independent government of planters, monopolizing all the land, the wealth, the education and the
respectability, was made nearly thirty years ago, with
J. C. Calhoun for a leader, and the question of slavery
was then only incidental. It was State rights and free
trade, not slavery, that called out the cockades, which
the firm purpose and true national devotion of Jackson
so soon suppressed, but did not extinguish. The prejudice of the poor whites of the South had not then
been aroused, and only the aristocracy could be enlisted
in the movement. They soon saw their weakness, and

only abandoned the movement temporarily, till they could find a suitable subject, and have time to arouse the prejudices of the poor, so as to band an army when the next move should be made.

The leaders in that movement having discovered that it would require physical as well as intellectual force to get out of the Union and destroy the government, slavery was the best subject with which to awaken a prejudice, because all the poor whites could understand it, and *felt* that they were superior to *all* laborers, black or white; and to be reduced to *laborers* was about or quite equal to being reduced to slavery; and, by convincing them that in the North the poor whites were laborers, and that northern society would soon make them so, and thus reduce them to the grade of slaves, was sufficient argument to arouse them even to the fighting pitch, which in that climate borders closely on prejudice and anger. The leading aristocrats have taken ample time to do this, and prevented all northern speakers from exposing them and enlightening the people on their true interests and their relation to slavery and labor.

4. It has been currently reported, and is no doubt true, that the leaders of the rebellion have offered to sacrifice slavery, and to abolish it gradually, or at once, for a foreign recognition, and such assistance as would enable them to establish a nationality; and, it is said, even offered to establish a monarchy, with a titled aristocracy, and without slavery, for the aid of France and England to free them from their allegiance to the odious democratic government of the United States; showing plainly that it was not slavery, but this monopoly and aristocracy, they were in rebellion to sustain, and

that their greatest enemy was the democracy of free
land, free labor, and free schools.

5. Many men and women are to be found, both South
and North, who sympathize with and aid all they can
the rebellion, who have never owned slaves, and never
would own one, and who have not even a friendship for
slavery, but call it a curse, and would at any time vote
to extinguish it; but these are invariably persons who,
by birth, or education, or wealth, or all of them, have
their feelings deeply interested in and imbued with
aristocracy and exclusive privileges.

6. It has been long since established, in political
economy, that, where the land and wealth and education can be monopolized, the poor, whether white or
black, can be kept in poverty, servitude and labor by
the rich, and made as useful and obedient, and their
labor engrossed as effectually, without a property in
their persons as with; and this being the determined
condition of society in the South, they could use the
laborers as profitably without owning them as with.
There is no doubt that nearly as much profit is made
by the property owners in England, from the laborers
who own themselves, and are controlled by the rich
through poverty, as from the slaves of the cotton and
sugar planters, except, perhaps, that it is cheaper to
feed and clothe in the cotton States, and hence a less
per cent. is to be deducted for that purpose. It is said
the laborers of England are allowed twenty-five per
cent. of their earnings to subsist on. The slaves probably do not consume over ten or fifteen per cent. of
theirs, and perhaps on some of the largest cotton plantations not even that. They could therefore carry on
the government of a southern aristocracy without

slavery, and gain the main points in the rebellion as effectually without it as with it.

7. The leading rebels have labored to produce, and succeeded in producing, in the minds of the poor whites, more prejudice against northern free laborers than against slaves and slave labor; and, without any reason, the poor whites of the South are made both to despise and hate the laborers of the North, whose condition is a hundred times superior to their own, while they have at least no prejudice against the slaves, or, if they have, it is not because they labor — the prejudice being against *free* laborers only, and got up wholly by an aristocracy to aid in setting up a government which could continue to rob the poor, both white and black, of the products of their labor, and of their natural rights. To maintain an aristocracy, it was necessary to monopolize all that was valuable; and to do this with slavery, this prejudice against free labor must be maintained, else the free laborers would acquire wealth, and then education, and be up in a social condition with the heirs of old estates. While the leaders had created this prejudice to maintain the rebellion, they were ready to sacrifice slavery, and enter all the negroes as free laborers, and of course put them on a level with the poor whites, if they could, by so doing, sustain their effort to establish an aristocracy, and prevent democracy in their society.

8. The slave trade is not more wicked or morally odious than slavery itself, and is one natural and legitimate feeder of the system, and to a slaveholding nation would be equally profitable and appropriate as a part of its commerce, especially if, as some contend, slavery is an institution to civilize and christianize barbarians,

and fit them for freedom; and yet the rebels readily give up the slave trade, and resolve against it — at least sufficient to hold in the rebellion the slave-breeders of Virginia, Kentucky and Tennessee, and the Quakers of North Carolina and Georgia; because it is aristocracy and not slavery they are fighting for, and democracy and not tyranny they are fighting against. All their resolves and reasons for secession were as false, futile and groundless as those on the slave trade, because they dare not openly and boldly declare the true reasons for the rebellion, lest their poor and middle classes of whites should abandon them, and they have leaders without an army, or a congress without supporters. Were slavery the cause of the rebellion, they could as openly and justly defend the slave trade as slave labor, and the whole system would stand or fall together.

9. The efforts of some planters, who were wholly devoted to slavery, have failed in most of the South to expel the free blacks, and confine the whole race to slavery, although this was seen to be necessary to its perpetuity; and they have also failed, although often carrying legislative enactments with them, in preventing the partial education of some slaves, and the emancipation of some, also; both of which were wearing away slavery, especially when the slave trade was cut off. While these slow but sure signs of ultimate emancipation were going on, the planters were all united in preventing free schools for the poor white children, the organization and adoption of white labor, and also a division of lands to the poor. They would as soon let a northern speaker declare the right of the slave to vote his freedom, as to declare the northern doctrine of "vote yourself a farm," which for a time was so prev-

alent in the Western States. They feared more the progress of democracy than the progress of abolition. They would as soon tolerate an abolitionist as an agent of Massachusetts (Mr. Hoar), who was only to look after the rights of northern *free* laborers in Charleston.

10. The constant demand of slaveholders for the privilege of carrying slavery into, or on to, new territory was merely a pretext for monopolizing the soil of such territories, and setting up a prejudice against free labor and small homesteads; for only a small portion of the old slave States has yet been cultivated, and those already in the Union were ample for slavery, if the slave trade was not reöpened, for at least one or two hundred years. Slavery has not succeeded in settling and developing the resources of Florida, Texas, Arkansas and Louisiana; and Missouri would have been equally behind but for the free labor that was rapidly crowding slavery out; while Michigan, Wisconsin, Illinois, Iowa and Minnesota have, notwithstanding their severe climate, been rapidly unfolding and gaining a place beside the oldest States in wealth, population, and representation in Congress. The cry for more slave territory was not for want of room for slavery, but to restrict democracy and extend aristocracy.

These and other evidences which might be produced seem to me conclusive against the opinion that slavery is the only or the main cause of the rebellion; but, at the same time, I freely admit that slavery was the exciting and inciting cause of the prejudice on the part of the southern population,—without which I do not know what subject they could have used, if any, of sufficient power to produce the result. It is doubtful if the leaders could have made more than a paper rebellion of resolutions, without the prejudice aroused on and by slavery both North and South; and equally so whether we could have put down a paper rebellion, if well managed, as easily as this one of armed force, and certainly not as effectually and finally.

I have no doubt that this will go into history as the "slaveholders' rebellion," and very properly so, for they were the main body of the leaders, and most slaveholders are aristocrats, but not all, for some, both in the cotton and the corn States, are among the most loyal families. That superficial observers will be led by this title to misunderstand the true issues, I have no doubt, as thousands have been from the constant and oft-repeated assertions of abolitionists, that slavery is the sole cause of all these troubles.

In suppressing the rebellion, no heed should be given to slavery, except so far as to protect deserting slaves, as we would other deserters, and never return them to any power that would restrain their freedom. Of course the government could not hold them as slaves, nor *recognize* them as slaves, and it is bound to protect them as citizens of the United States, when they come and ask its protection, the same as it would the poor white soldiers of the South when they come. The true policy was set forth in an order of one of the officers to his men: "If you see a slave standing, let him stand; if you see one running, let him run." Slavery is a social evil and a domestic institution, not a national; and the less the national government has to do with it the better, except to guard against and prohibit it, as it would polygamy.

I cannot approve the measure of paying from the national treasury for slaves in a State which has found

5

slavery an evil, and wishes to get rid of it, as the border
States really have, and would admit but for pride.  It
seems to me like hiring a man to take the medicine that
will cure him, or buying the horses and cattle of the
farmers that are worse than useless to them, when they
have already paid for themselves several times over.
By what principle of justice the honest laborers of the
North can be taxed to buy worthless property in Kentucky, I do not see; and most surely, if it is not property, we should not purchase it.  That many lazy and
noisy philanthropists, who do nothing and earn nothing,
should advocate it, is not surprising; but how those
who study the interest of the whole country can, is
beyond my comprehension.  Still we have borne worse
evils than this, and *can* pay for the slaves if we want to
abolish slavery.  If it is to purchase loyalty, it will
prove a poor investment; if it is to aid humanity, it
will prove as fruitless as the various missionary schemes
of the churches — great outlay and small gain to the
Lord or the race.

It is for the interest of Missouri, Arkansas, Texas,
Kentucky, Tennessee, Virginia, Maryland, Delaware,
and North Carolina, to abolish slavery at once, for several reasons.  1st. Because in these States most of the
slaves are prepared for freedom, and capable of supporting themselves.  2d. Slavery is not profitable in those
States, except in Arkansas and Texas, and there it is a
great detriment to the rapid settlement of the States by
free laborers.  3d. The States would at once gain, in -
the rise of real estate, more than the value of the slaves,
and far more rapidly develop their resources, by the
enterprise of free laborers and free schools.

The true policy is to extinguish the rebellion, and

extend the principles of the North over the slave States by every constitutional aid to free land, family home-steads, free labor, and free schools, and let them remove slavery by their influence on the State; which they would soon do if left to the whole people of the several States. This peaceable manner is far better for all par-ties than a hasty and revolutionary one, or a purchase and pay one.

As slavery was not the cause of the rebellion, so it should not be made the issue. But it will, no doubt, fall with the rebellion, even in the loyal States, or at least it will lose forever its power over the national government, and even its respectability and influence in the slave States will be gone forever, and then it will soon perish, for it cannot subsist under the contempt of the whole world. It has flourished mainly by its con-trol of our national affairs.

It is not strange that fanatics, and persons who live in passional excitement, should seize this hour of nation-al trial and trouble to press forward injudicious and hasty schemes of abolition, or emancipation, or coloniza-tion; but it is strange that men of sober minds and good sound practical judgment can be drawn into such meas-ures at such times, and when we have all we can attend to of more vital importance—namely, to keep what we have gained by our national government, and hold juris-diction over the land, and maintain the principles we have set up. When we have this quarrel settled, and this work done, it will be time enough to undertake anoth-er measure, and settle another question. Still, *if* slavery be made the issue for a division of our country, or na-tionality entire, with all intact, I would say, strike it out at once. If it is even necessary to save the Union, abol-

ish it in every State which has abolished the constitution
that secured it to them, and let their own poison kill
their favorite system.* They have no claim to a *constitutional* protection, as the loyal States have. Yet I do not
see the necessity or expediency of arbitrarily abolish-
ing it where they are not prepared, nor of buying them
where they are. I think we had better pay our debts;
give lands to the poor, both black and white; build more
school-houses for *all* children, and encourage white and
free labor; sustain schools, pupils, speakers and authors
over the whole Union; and thus sap the institution,
while we are by this means preparing both white and
black for freedom.

While I admit the correctness of the principles of the
abolitionists, and all the rights they claim for the slave,
and acknowledge all rights in slaves which I claim for
myself (for I was once a slave in New England, and
sold, by the overseers of the poor, at the age of four,
for sixteen years), yet I deprecate the religious fanati-
cism and overwrought zeal which constantly carry
them beyond reason, humanity, national welfare, and
practical measures of relief for either slave or master,
and which have furnished a good share of the ground-
work and arguments for the aristocrats of the South to
use in getting up this rebellion, and the prejudice
necessary as fuel to carry it on. Abolitionist has long
been the most odious term that could be applied to a
man in the cotton States, and even the poor lazy whites,
who had no slaves, no land, no education, no labor, no
respectability, "no nothing," would turn out to mob or
rob an abolitionist; and, in some districts of the North,

* Since the above was written, the proclamation has been issued, which I
fully endorse. — AUTHOR.

a slaveholder was nearly as odious; but the people being mostly educated above mobs, it was not unsafe for slaveholders to travel there and discover the state of feeling for themselves.

———◆———

## THE PRESS.

———

No instrument, except slavery, has been so potent in getting up this rebellion as the press, and no instrument so potent in putting it down. Like the breath of the traveller in the old fable, it warms the fingers and cools the broth, thus blowing hot and cold from the same mouth, to the astonishment of the ignorant peasant. The abolition press had long been heated to a glow, but could not get a weld to either party, for want of sufficient heat in them. The terrific blowing of the southern editors soon carried many of their papers beyond a welding heat, and, in a liquid state, they ran out over the ignorant masses, read at the street corners, and in bar-rooms (which, in the absence of school-houses, were very numerous); and thus the southern people were educated on the character of the Yankees, and abolitionists, and the North generally, by the most potent instrument of education used in civilization, and which has been mainly in the hands of the most reckless and unscrupulous set of editors that could be raised from the whole nation, often without regard to literary ability, but with sufficient talent and recklessness to write

5*

without the least regard to truth, whatever would incite
and excite the poor deluded masses of robbed whites
to aid in the rebellion that was, if successful, to end in
their ruin to the third or fourth generation, at least.

I will insert one extract here, which is of the same
character as scores which I have read, and hundreds of
which have been published and circulated in the South,
where the people could get no evidence of their falsehood because debarred entirely, by poverty and ignorance and other barriers, from all correct and reliable
information on the subject. Those who could read did
not dare read to them the truth, if they had it, which
few had or could get, especially after the rebellion
broke out. I cut it from the *Missouri Democrat*, of
March, 1862.

"A HIGH OLD ARTICLE FROM THE RICHMOND WHIG.

"We must say, in explanation of the second paragraph of the following
article, that it was written before the *Richmond Whig* had heard from
Roanoke Island, and Forts Henry and Donelson. Its belief in the superiority of southern soldiers over the Yankees has probably been modi-
fied.

"QUANTITY VS. QUALITY.

"About 1850, when the great north-eastern deluge, of which mention
has been made, swept over our commonwealth, and laid waste our long
cherished institutions, it was very much the fashion for the 'dear friend
of the people,' to hold up the Yankees as the models of every virtue. They
were the thriftiest, the shrewdest, the cutest, the most enterprising, the
most industrious, and the most money-getting people in the world. But
their wealth, their stinginess, their venality, their dexterity in swindling
and unscrupulousness in lying, all paled before their unmatchable fecun-
dity. Behold how they multiply! They are as multitudinous as the stars
in the heavens or the sand on the sea-shore. Malthus, never a favorite
with the sentimentalist, though teeming with the profoundest wisdom, was
universally discarded as a humbug and charlatan. The great Yankee
nation, which doubled itself every five years, was the true exemplar of all
political science, and the only model of political greatness. It is very

true that the Yankees are, without a doubt, eminently endowed with the procreative faculty. Their men are lecherous as monkeys; and the women, scraggy, scrawny, and hard as whip-cord, breed like Norway rats, and they fill all the brothels on the continent. It is not presumable that the tender emotions of love ever penetrate their bony bosoms; but they indulge passion because it smacks of the savor of forbidden fruit, which is sweet to their sinful natures. But they multiply — the only scriptural precept they obey — and boast their millions. So do the Chinese; so do the Apsidæ, and all other pests of the animal kingdom. Pull the bark from a decayed log, and you will see a mass of maggots — full of vitality, in constant motion and eternal gyration, one crawling over one, and another creeping under another — all precisely alike, all intently engaged in preying upon one another — and you have an apt illustration of Yankee numbers, Yankee equality, and Yankee prowess.

"This war will test the physical virtues of mere numbers. Southern soldiers ask no better odds than one to three of the Western, and one to six of the Eastern Yankees. Some go so far as to say that, with equal weapons and on equal grounds, they would not hesitate to encounter twenty times their number of the last. In respect to administrative talent, the world has never seen such a failure. With a government thoroughly organized to their hands, complete in all its branches, they have well-nigh smashed the whole concern in less than twelve months. So numbers do not make either warriors or statesmen.

"In regard to the moral, the effects are by no means encouraging. We doubt if any society, since that of Sodom and Gomorrah, has ever been more thoroughly steeped in every species of vice than that of the Yankees. Infanticide is one of the established customs of the oriental Chinese; and it is by no means certain that it has not extensive prevalence among their brethren of the moral North. But this imputation need not be laid to their charge— they are bad enough without it. There is no one virtue cherished among them, except money-getting, if that can be called a virtue, pursued as it is by them to the stifling of every sentiment of generosity and honor. With envy and malignity, they pursue every excellence that shows itself among them, unconnected with money; and a gentleman there stands no more chance of existence than a dog does in the Grotto del Cano."

I could copy other articles from Charleston, S. C., or Memphis, Tenn., papers, even worse than this; but this is as low in language as I can allow in my book, and as false and scurrilous as I wish to exhibit. These are almost conclusive evidence of my position in regard to the tyrants' hatred of our northern democracy, and show plainly what they were fighting for.

Nothing less than such battles as those of Mill Spring and Donelson, Springfield, Missouri, and Pea Ridge, Arkansas, and the naval feats of Hilton Head, New Orleans and Memphis, could disabuse the people of the South of opinions formed from these lying sheets. These sheets, as soon as our army reaches their respective localities, will pass into loyal hands, with new editors, as the lying and slanderous ones skedaddle. Where they will go and what they will do, I know not, but probably most of them will turn slave-drivers in the cotton and cane fields and rice swamps, if slavery continues there, and prove as reckless in driving slaves as they were for a time in driving quills. But I think the editors of the *Richmond Whig* and *Memphis Avalanche* would be more valuable in Barnum's Museum, for a few years, if well patched over with their own editorials.

The leaders of the southern rebellion took especial pains to have the southern press in the hands of editors truly loyal to them, and also to have, as far as possible, desperate, reckless, and intellectual editors, several of whom were raised in the North. The national government had no control of the press, direct or indirect, until after the rebellion had broken out. Where the people were loyal, many of the papers had to stop or exchange hands and editors; and then the government, with the most loyal people and press, had much trouble to prevent the rebels from getting useful information from our papers, through their eagerness to feed a reading, earnest and loyal community.

The press is inestimable in value in a country like ours, with democratic institutions; but, like fire in the hands of an incendiary, may also be made to do great mischief. Such the southern press has been made to do, and, in some cases, a portion of the northern press also; yet, as we would not dispense with or restrict fire because incendiaries use it, so we would not hamper or restrict the press because wicked men often use it for the worst and basest of purposes. It must and will go with our system of democracy, and go *free*.

## THE PULPIT.

### PRAYER-MEETING IN A STORM.

#### BY BAYARD TAYLOR.

[See President Buchanan's last Proclamation.]

A GALE came up from the sou'-sou'-west;
  'T was fierce November weather;
But the ship had felt such a storm before,
  And her planks still held together.
And thus, though the howling tempest showed
  No signs of diminution,
The passengers said, " We 'll trust our ship,
  The staunch old Constitution ! "

The captain stood on the quarter-deck;
  " The seas," he said, " they batter us.
'T was my watch below in the former gale;
  I doubt if we 'll weather Hatteras.
The wind on the one side blows me off,
  The current sets me shoreward;
I 'll just lay-to between them both,
  And *seem* to be going forward."

" Breakers ahead ! " cried the watch on the bow ;
    " Hard up ! " was the first mate's order ;
" She feels the ground-swell," the passengers cried,
    " And the seas already board her ! "
The foresail split in the angry gust ;
    In the hold the ballast shifted ;
And an old tar said, " If Jackson steered,
    We should n't thus have drifted ! "

But the captain cried, " Let go your helm ! "
    And then he called to the bo'swain, —
" Pipe all hands to the quarter-deck,
    And we 'll save her by Devotion ! "
The first mate hurled his trumpet down ;
    The old tars cursed together,
To see the good ship helpless roll
    At the sport of wave and weather.

The tattered sails are all a-back ;
    Yards crack, and masts are started ;
And the captain weeps and says his prayers,
    Till the hull be 'midships parted.
But God is on the steersman's side ;
    The crew are in revolution ;
The wave that washes the captain off
    Will save the Constitution !

NEW YORK, DEC. 1860.

THE pulpit, like the press, has also done its share in
producing and suppressing rebellion. It has been a
ready and willing instrument in the hands of the aristocrats,—even more subservient to them than to the
democracy,—and fully proved its recreancy to the
beautiful democratic precepts and practices of Jesus.
In fact, the last fifty years have very nearly proved that
we have no genuine Christianity, and few, if any, true
followers of Jesus. His religion was a pure democracy, — ours, nearly all a petty aristocracy, with exclusive privileges, and better adapted to southern chivalry

than to northern democracy. Hence, tho southern pulpit, religion and all, was fully enlisted in tho most wicked rebellion against tho rights, interests and welfare of tho whole people. The people will lose all confidence in the pulpit when a few such evidences are exhibited of its want of religion and humanity.

I could have selected some specimens of rebel sermons, and put them beside those of Beecher and Chapin, and easily shown that brother was warring on brother, both of the same religious belief, on the road to tho same heaven, fighting as they go, and abusing each other as bad as the most wicked politicians; but I refrain from such sacrilegious task, and turn to the political parties.

———◆———

## POLITICAL PARTIES.

———

It was, no doubt, the intention and expectation of the leading rebels to use, at least, one political party to carry out their plans, as they had often done to carry elections and to control the national government; and they had been shrewd enough to unite long before with the northern party known as the Democratic party, and which once had more democracy than any other party, but which latterly became corrupt under southern leaders, and often pandered to aristocracy, and yielded its best and most sacred principles. This induced many of its best and truest members to abandon it, and start, or join, a "Free soil" party, which slid into the

Republican, with a large amount of "floodwood and fragments" of the old Whig party. The old Whig party had been so often beaten that it had become discouraged and broken up, scattering its fragments in various groups of Abolitionists, Native Americans, Republicans, Southern Rights, &c.

The democracy had become so effectually split, in the presidential contest of 1860, between the traitor Breckenridge and the true and loyal Douglas (than whom a more devoted friend of the nation was not to be found in any party), that the rebels lost control over it, and, when they set their faces to overthrow the government, they found some of the leading northern Democrats first and foremost in the field and council, and wielding the most potent weapons of tongue, pen and sword, no doubt to their great disappointment, especially when many who supported Breckenridge were found among them. Most of the northern Democrats were as loyal as Republicans to the nation, and a Butler, a Dix, a Dickenson, and even an Everett, were among the first in the field with tongues and pens, or swords, ready to sustain the President. A few fragments of all parties in the North were in sympathy with the aristocracy, and some with slavery; but these were insignificant, and soon were subdued and made ashamed of their sympathy with treason.

A close examination of the rebellion will exculpate all political parties, and prove that this was not a political rebellion, but a social one, and that, had the Democrats elected Douglas, the rebels would have moved as surely as with Lincoln, but weaker in the border States, —weaker only because Douglas had more personal friends in the slave States; but the issues would have been the same,—Aristocracy against Democracy—the few against the many—cotton against corn.

No fragments of the old parties will be collected on old issues, or by old leaders, when the rebels are subdued; but two great parties will stand,—one in defence of capital, and the other of labor. Partially aristocracy and democracy, respectability and sectarian religion, will set up an aristocracy, and equal rights and respect for all will contend with it; slavery will lose its power, and anti-slavery its edge; the former will die out, and the latter, of course, follow after. Once dead, it will be buried below a resurrection. No one will ask Ben Butler or Jim Lane whom he voted for in 1860, but what *are* your principles? No credit or odium will attach to any person for any party action or vote previous to the rebellion; but loyalty and treason will adhere to persons and families for the part taken in the rebellion, without reference to political antecedents. The hearts of the people are truly democratic, and, if not deceived, will meet tyranny and aristocracy with a bold and united front. The working people everywhere should belong to a democratic party, and all unite to secure land, labor and education for all, both male and female, black, white and red, and the equal rights of franchise, etc., for women as for men. When that party organizes, my tongue and pen are ready for service.

Neither the pulpit, nor press, nor old political parties, are true to democracy and the interests of the people; but if the workers are educated, they will be true to themselves, and thus save the country.

6

# BANKS.

BANKS are not made for the poor, nor for the good of laborers, but for the rich, and to aid aristocracy. The poor are often made to believe banks are created to make money plenty, and greatly to their advantage; but it is never so. They aid to enhance the price of land, and to secure the profits of labor to the rich, and not to the poor, and hence are usually the instruments of aristocrats.

A new system of banking, recently published by Lysander Spooner, of Boston, would bring these instruments nearer to the people than any I have ever read · but all corporations which monopolize land or money, are, by their very nature, against the interests of the people, especially the poor. The true policy of a democratic government is to make a metallic currency, and make it the basis of all money circulation; issue its evidences of debt (treasury notes) for its liabilities, and receive these for taxes, lands, postage, and all sums due the State or individuals that are collected by the laws for the maintenance of government of the nation or State; and, beyond this, if more currency is needed, let any improvements in real-estate be represented in paper, and transferable by record and endorsement by a proper officer, and thus allow the poor man to have one hundred dollars of currency in circulation as good as the ten thousand dollars of the rich in proportion to its quantity.

Especial privileges are always opposed to democracy;.

hence general laws should be resorted to, whenever they can be, instead of especial. It is true the banks in the loyal States assisted the nation in its crisis; the banks of the rebellious States, also, as readily aided the rebels as far as in their power, in each case seeking their own pecuniary gain. An immense profit was made from the government by the banks of the great cities in the loyal States, under pretence of aiding the government; and had it not been for the foresight, integrity and democracy of Secretary Chase and a few leading men in Congress, and their success in securing the treasury note law, with its legal tender feature, they would have rendered the government bankrupt, and had the whole currency under their control, and proved a monopoly ten times worse than ever the U. S. Bank was. No wonder all true democrats are opposed to banks, for they oppress the people.

## THE FUGITIVE SLAVE LAW.

THIS exceedingly unpopular statute, having been rendered as odious and offensive as possible to the North by the southern leaders, if not, indeed, unconstitutional (which I believe it was), was rendered obnoxious to the people, who are superior to all law, and thus was annulled and fell a dead letter at the outbreak of this rebellion, doing no further service for any party, and leaving no hope of its resurrection. It may now as well be repealed as to longer disgrace our national statute books.

That this law had some influence in creating a national prejudice, and aided in getting up the rebellion, there is no doubt; but when the rebellion came, it was worthless to all parties.

If there are guaranties in the constitution to slaveholders, there are just and proper modes of carrying them out without doing such injustice to humanity as the authors of that instrument never dreamed of.

There is no need of outraging human nature and justice both to carry out a democratic constitution; and certainly no person can constitutionally defend the justice or humanity of that law. It will long remain a black mark on our national escutcheon, and should be expunged.

---

# GARRISONIANISM.

That the Garrisonians have done some wind-work in blowing up the rebellion, no one can doubt; but, as they did not vote, and were non-resistants in principle, and true to their principles generally, they certainly cannot be charged with a belligerent disposition or design. They sought the abolition of slavery by moral power, but were often exceedingly bitter and abusive on the slaveholders, and often had more sympathy for the slaves than for their masters, who, on a long line of observation and charity, deserve as much, if not more; for the masters would certainly be destroyed by slavery in the end; and they were still more apt to leave the poor whites of the slave States out in the cold, without the common sympathy of humanity, which was extended profusely to the slave.

No person, acquainted as I am with the leading Garrisonians, can fail to credit them with good hearts, and good motives, however much he may find of policy to condemn. I have always thought they should vote, and take part in reforming the bad government, and fight, too, when necessary to save all we have gained, as a basis to build a higher and better structure on. "Give the devil his due," and abolitionists, too. The abolitionists have a deep and true principle at the bottom, and plead for humanity, if often too zealously; while the fire-eaters have only hatred and revenge in return for principles.

## KNIGHTS OF THE GOLDEN CIRCLE.

THAT a secret organization, with the above name, did exist in the South, and tied the hands and tongues of a few politicians in the North, I have good reason to believe; but I have not been able to procure a copy of the little book said to contain a part of their principles and regulations. I have seen one said to be such, but it was evidently a forgery.

That the whole design was treason, is evident from the fact that it was kept entirely secret till the rebellion gave a protection to its members, and then it came to light only in time to share the fate of the rebellion, and brand its members with one of the blackest political crimes of civilization.

Entirely unlike abolitionism,—which sought exposure, discussion, controversy, and its enemies, with a determination to subdue them by moral force,—whether it could or not, the Knights of the Golden Circle did not dare meet them in argument, and openly compare principles and rights, interests, and duties.

Treason seeks secrecy and silence, deception and falsehood; but loyalty needs no cover, patriotism no shield, and human rights no conspiracy, although often driven to rebellion against usurpers and tyranny. This Golden Circle may prove a circle for communications of evil spirits.

---

# FOREIGN SYMPATHY.

---

## "THE STRENGTH OF TYRANNY.

" The tyrant's chains are only strong
   While slaves submit to wear them ;
And who could bind them on the throng
   Determined not to bear them?
Then clank your chains — e'en though the links
   Were light as fashion's feather,
The heart which rightly feels and thinks
   Would cast them altogether.

" The lords of earth are only great
   While others clothe and feed them !
But what were all their pride and state
   Should labor cease to feed them?
The swain is higher than a king ; —
   Before the laws of Nature,

The monarch were a useless thing,
   The swain a useful creature.

" We toil, we spin, we delve the mine,
   Sustaining each his neighbor ;
And who can hold a right divine
   To rob us of our labor ?
We rush to battle — bear our lot
   In every ill and danger ;
And who shall make the peaceful cot
   To homely joy a stranger ?

"Perish all tyrants far and near,
   Beneath the chains that bind us ;
And perish, too, that servile fear
   Which makes the slaves they find us.
One grand, one universal claim —
   One peal of moral thunder —
One glorious burst in Freedom's name,
   And rend our bonds asunder ! ' '

No doubt great dependence was placed by the rebels
on foreign aid and sympathy ; and well might they rely
on it ; for, although they could not expect sympathy
for slavery, or aid in sustaining it, or permission to re-
open the slave trade, still they could rely on aristocratic
aid and sympathy for the aristocracy of the cotton
States, even with slavery attached to them. The *aristocracy* of Europe is not opposed to slavery ; but the
united public sentiment of the great body of the people
in civilized nations has forced it out of Europe ; and it
is this sentiment of the poor laboring masses that com-
pels the action of the European governments, which are
consequently against slavery, while the landlords and
title-lords are in full sympathy with the cotton aristocrats and plantation lords of the rebellious States.

A monarchy, with a titled aristocracy, would far better suit the South than a democracy. The planters

would sooner take the chance of being graded up to nobility, than be graded down to labor and small farms, to universal suffrage, and equal rights, and free schools. Of course, in this they would have the aid and comfort, sympathy and assistance, of the noble lords of Europe.

The British government felt of its public pulse to ascertain how far it could aid the rebels; but Napoleon knew the state of feeling without feeling the pulse of France; and both found the people were in close sympathy with the free States, and with the national government, as far as they knew its objects and principles; and these they knew too well, to be wrong or far misled. With this condition of their people and public sentiment, they could lend only private sympathy and money; but the latter they would not lend, because they could not afford to risk it in so desperate a game, for they well knew the chance of its return was very small.

As might have been easily foreseen, the rebels could get all the aid and comfort that aristocratic sympathy and newspaper puffs could furnish from Europe, but little or no money, and no national recognition. The cotton-spinners of Manchester might lack cotton for a few months, but, if they knew the true issue, they would go hungry sooner than aid a rebellion that was to work a perpetual ruin to laborers and their posterity; and the free speech of England would allow them and all other laborers to learn the facts and true issue.

I insert here an article from a July number of the *New York Times*.

"ENGLISH AND AMERICAN ARISTOCRACY.

"Two events have occured recently in England, which are significant of the state of public feeling toward America. On the annual Commemoration Day of the Founders of Oxford, the students are in the habit, before the usual address is delivered, of cheering and hissing the different names of popular or odious public men as they are proposed. The name of GARIBALDI had been cheered, and that of NAPOLEON both cheered and hissed, when some one shouted out the name of 'JEFFERSON DAVIS;' it was received with tumultuous and unanimous applause. 'PRESIDENT LINCOLN' was proposed, and it was greeted with hisses and groans.

"The other incident to which we allude, was the public meeting, already described in our columns, of the operatives in Manchester ; the hard-working, pinched, hungry masses of men in the cotton and other manufactures of that city. They were called together to hear a proposal from a Member of Parliament, that the English Government should intervene in the American civil war — nominally for the sake of peace, but really to establish the Southern Confederacy. These men had been the great sufferers from our war ; their wives and children were crying vainly at home for bread to feed them, while all their aristocratic teachers assured them they had but to acknowledge the South, and cotton would pour in its stream of labor and wealth to them. They had heard it continually from the higher classes, that the only object of the North was power and territory, and that the South were but asserting the rights of the Declaration of Independence, and struggling for liberty. With these fallacies before them, with hunger and want behind them, the operatives of Manchester reversed the whole object of the meeting ; rejected the proposition of Mr. HOPWOOD; passed a motion with immense applause, in favor of preserving the American Union and supporting the policy of President LINCOLN.

"We would not exaggerate the importance of either of these events — certainly not of the first. Still they may be considered as straws on the surface of English opinion. The instinct of portions of the people, has struck through to the essential character of our civil war. The sons of the aristocracy — those whose fathers and ancestors have become rich and powerful, either by burdens laid on the people or by wealth taken from them; who dread, beyond all things, the equal elevation of the masses with themselves ; who hate the very name of Democracy — these naturally feel for the so-called aristocrats of America — the nobility of the slave-pen and plantation. They feel unconsciously, or they have heard it at home, that the same struggle is raging on American soil which has convulsed Europe and will convulse it again — the struggle between those who would raise up the lowest classes to the rights and privileges of humanity, and those who would depress them for their own base purposes.

"They see well that the stupendous conflict which is desolating a continent is no causeless and unmeaning struggle, but is indeed the clashing

of principles; that this, even as the first French Revolution, is essentially
a war of Democracy against privilege; for the rights of man against the
immunities of a class. The triumph of the North would be the triumph
of Democracy, and they dread it (very reasonably) almost as they would
a revolution of the British masses themselves. The success of the South
would be the ruin of the American-Republican experiment, and would
throw back the popular party in Europe for a century; therefore they
pray for it and cheer its rebellious leader. They are perfectly right and
reasonable. The victory of the North would give a shock to aristocratic
privileges in England, from which they would never recover. Reform,
popular suffrage, the abolition of a State-Church, the elevation of the
working classes, would be, in the future, the possible English results of
our success. No wonder that the boys of the universities shout for a
Slaveholding Confederacy and the great repudiator.

"On the other hand, a portion of the working classes—those who
think for themselves—feel at once that the national cause in America and
the popular cause in England are one. Though temporarily we deprive
them of bread, with a noble instinct they feel that we are really striking
for them and the rights of mankind against caste and power. As Mr.
LINCOLN said in his message, 'they know that the destruction of the
American Republic—whatever else it may mean—means no good to the
common people.' While an army of the middle classes are hoodwinked
by the aristocracy, or are blinded by national jealousy and selfishness, not
looking under the surface of events here and seeing the real struggle of
great ideas beneath party cries and official proclamations, the heart of the
English discern the truth as by instinct. They see in the southern leaders
not merely oppressors of the negro, but oppressors of mankind. The
victory of our government is to them the victory of Universal Suffrage, of
Republicanism, Liberty and Justice to the poor; all for which the people
have struggled so long in Europe. The triumph of the South is, to their
clear vision, the triumph of a privileged few — the basest aristocracy ever
formed, conspicuous for ferocity, cruelty and meanness — grown rich on
the sale of human bodies, and fattened by the blood of the poor."

There was an attempt made to deceive the people of
Europe with the idea that the issue was slavery and its
perpetuity. This was made mostly by abolitionists; no
doubt honestly in most cases, for many of them believed
it, being themselves deceived in the issues; but the
southern visitors and commissioners soon disabused

them, and gave the true issues by promising to sacrifice slavery for assistance,—not aware, it seems, that
the laborers of Europe had so much influence over the
governments as to prevent the aid and recognition they
expected, when the truth became known to them. Both
parties were deceived,—the abolitionists in expecting
to find a universal sentiment and prejudice against
slavery, and the cotton lords in expecting the rich aristocrats had absolute sway in the governments of Europe. Both have learned a lesson, and may be wiser in
the future. The sympathy without assistance comes to
the South from the rich; and the sympathy without the
assistance (which was not needed nor asked for) from
the laborers comes to the North, but not from a prejudice against slavery. They seem to understand and
appreciate the true issues better than many of our own
citizens. They either did not read, or were not deceived by, the Count Gasparin's book on the uprising of
a great people, which, with all its beauty of diction and
many facts, had the fundamental error of placing slavery
at the bottom of the rebellion, when aristocracy, with
monopolizing power and exclusive privileges, was
its foundation, as any person ought to have known at
least from the character of foreign sympathy, if from no
other evidence.

The South is about as far behind the most advanced
nations of Europe as the North is in advance in its democracy; hence the laborers of Europe would favor the
North, and the rich the South, with such aid and comfort as they could safely invest. All the North required
was for Europe to attend to its own affairs, and not
meddle with our domestic troubles, which we are fully
able to settle among ourselves. But the South de-

pended on the aristocratic powers of the Old World to aid them in overthrowing the democracy of the New; and, when disappointed in securing it, were already half defeated.

## CONSISTENCY.

IF "consistency is a jewel," it certainly has not been in possession of the Confederate Government; for while they have insisted on the right of South Carolina and Florida to leave the nation by the almost unanimous voice of the voters, they have persistently refused to let Kentucky and Missouri stay in the Union by an equally decisive vote; and while they contend for the rights of Eastern Virginia to leave the nation, and join its fortunes with the South, they deny the same right to Western Virginia to leave the State and stay in the nation. They ridicule the idea of any man representing parts of Tennessee or North Carolina in Congress, and yet have renegade politicians, who dare not appear in the States or districts they claim to represent, pretending to be members of the Confederate Congress from Kentucky, Missouri, etc.; and even talk of extending jurisdiction over Maryland, when Maryland herself would drive them from her soil as a band of robbers, as Kentucky and Missouri have already done, by the aid of the welcome soldiers from more northern States.

Another evidence of inconsistency was the appeal to England to raise the blockade, that she might supply herself with cotton, and, in the same appeal, asking her to break it because it is not efficient; when, if the latter were true, of course the cotton would be supplied, and there would be little or no cause for raising it; declaring the blockade inefficient and scarcely even annoying their vessels, and yet entreating foreign nations to raise it, but evidently to enlist them in its cause.

They have also constantly declared their ability to sustain themselves, and fight their way into nationality, and at the same time sent their most eloquent and influential men to Europe to solicit aid, and to make almost any sacrifice to obtain it; showing plainly that their boasting was only boasting, and that they knew their weakness and depended on foreign aid.

For many years they were ready to have a northern abolitionist hung, who should say a word in favor of dissolving the Union; then, all at once, they change fronts, and attempt to dissolve it, and justify themselves by the constitution; then, setting the constitution entirely aside, they constantly complain of the loyal States and government for violating it. While they feign to venerate Washington and Jefferson, they are using all their power to overthrow the government and principles founded by them and set in operation over North and South.

I could go on to mention scores of similar inconsistencies, but this will suffice.

# CONFEDERACY.

## REPUDIATION.

" 'NEATH a ragged palmetto a southerner sat,
A twisting the band of his Panama hat,
And trying to lighten his mind of a load,
By humming the words of the following ode :
    ' O for a nigger, and O for a whip !
    O for a cocktail, and O for a nip !
    O for a shot at old Greeley and Beecher !
    O for a crack at a Yankee school-teacher !
    O for a captain, and O for a ship !
    O for a cargo of niggers each trip ! '
And so he kept oh-ing for what he had not,
Not contented with owing for all that he'd got."

THE name and effort of confederacy is evidently a
ruse to gain time and strength, as an aristocracy and
monopoly, such as the rebels seek, could only be maintained by a consolidated government with absolute
power and a standing army.

It is evident they do not intend any State shall se-
cede from their government, nor that any slave State
shall stay out of the contest, if the others can bring
it in by persuasion or force. A temporary confederacy, to gain all they can from the border States, and
then a single State and consolidated government, with a
titled aristocracy and perpetual privileges secured to
families, and an army to maintain them, is, and was
from the first, the aim of the leaders of the rebellion,
leaving no root of the democracy, toward which they
have shown such hatred, and tried so hard to destroy.

Confederacy, like the rattlesnake flag, was only

adopted temporarily, to draw in and out certain aid that could not be secured without some show of the principles to which they had feigned so much attach- ment a few years before

---

# THE ARMY AND NAVY.

---

THAT the officers of the army and navy had long been toasted and flattered, feted and cajoled, by the southern aristocrats, we have the fullest evidence, and that many of them were thus impregnated with southern senti- ment, and ready for treason, was fully established at and before the outbreak; but not a single company of soldiers, and, so far as I have learned, not a soldier of the regular army, proved to be a traitor in the rebel- lion. The truth is, the South did not toast and fete them; it had no exclusive privileges for the soldier,— no pension, no land bounty, no rights; it asked them to fight for the glory of the officers and leaders, and, if successful, they should be kicked out of all decent society ever after; if beaten, they were no loss to the aristocrats, who had no interest in them, except as they could be used in battles as the slaves are on the planta- tions.

The soldiers of the regular army seemed to under- stand this; hence they could not be drawn or driven into the rebellion, while the officers were easily led, by the offers of luxury and honor, to join in the rebellion to overthrow the government that had educated, sustained, and often enriched them.

The same was true of the navy as of the army. Soldiers and seamen were true to the North and the government, and officers full of treason and disloyalty; showing plainly that the North was the friend of the soldier and seaman and laborer, and the South the friend of officers and leaders, aristocracy and wealth, as I have elsewhere shown.

------◆------

# THE UNDERGROUND RAILROAD.

It has passed into a proverb, that fugitive slaves run off from their masters, and escape North on the underground railroad,—meaning, by stealth and ·stealthy assistance; but all the complaints on this account made not one point in the causes of the rebellion. They did assist in arousing some southern prejudice against those who were supposed to assist in this secret business.

The last passenger on the underground railroad was President Lincoln, who went South instead of North, and thereby eluded the mob that intended to assassinate him, as effectually as many slaves eluded pursuit and escaped to Canada. Since his transit through Baltimore, on his way to the capital, the business of the underground road has been suspended, and the slaves, declared by Gen. Butler contraband of war, have taken the upper railroad and passed safely North.

There will be no further occasion for the road, and

hereafter "Othello's occupation is gone." Slaves ran North till a President ran South, and then slaves could walk North by daylight; and soon all citizens of the nation will be protected in all parts of the nation, and northern speakers can go South and teach truths the people there never have heard.

---

# CONCLUSION.

---

### "THREE HUNDRED THOUSAND MORE.

" WE are coming, Father Abraham, three hundred thousand more,
From Mississippi's winding stream, and from New England's shore ;
We leave our ploughs and workshops, our wives and children dear,
With hearts too full for utterance, with but a silent tear ;
We dare not look behind us, but steadfastly before —
We are coming Father Abraham — three hundred thousand more !

" If you look across the hill-tops that meet the Northern sky,
Lou̱ ⁻ⁱⁿ⁓ lines of rising dust your vision may descry ;
And now the wind, an instant, tears the cloudy veil aside,
And floats aloft our spangled flag in glory and in pride ;
And bayonets in the sunlight gleam, and bands brave music pour —
We are coming, Father Abraham — three hundred thousand more !

" If you look up all our valleys, where the growing harvests shine,
You may see our sturdy farmer boys fast forming into line ;
And children from their mothers' knees are pulling at the weeds,
And learning how to reap and sow, against their country's needs ;
And a farewell group stands weeping at every cottage door —
We are coming, Father Abraham — three hundred thousand more !

" You have called us, and we 're coming, by Richmond's bloody tide
To lay us down for Freedom's sake, our brothers' bones beside ;

7*

•

Or from foul treason's savage grasp to wrench the murderous blade,
And in the face of foreign foes its fragments to parade.
Six hundred thousand loyal men and true have gone before —
We are coming, Father Abraham — three hundred thousand more !

COTTON and corn have had a war, — cotton with slaves,
and corn with free laborers. Cotton is beaten, and corn
is king. Slavery dies, and free labor triumphs; property turns into persons — chattels into freemen; democracy triumphs over aristocracy; freeholders increase
from the ranks of the landless; laborers are more honorable than non-producers; education is free to all
children; science roots out superstition, and better and
more liberal laws are enacted by each State. The spin-
dles will be supplied, from the fingers of free laborers,
with cotton and flax and wool, as the workmen have
heretofore been with bread. The resources of the
great South will be developed by Yankee enterprise,
and the children of her poor will be rescued from the
withering damnation of poverty, ignorance and idleness.
"Excelsior," may be written on the laborer's banner,
and borne in triumph both North and South. No more
abolition hatred, and no more southern revenge. A
nation united in objects and purposes, and able to
defend itself against the world, — stretching from ocean
to ocean, from the torrid regions of the gulf, to the
frozen regions of the uppermost of the great lakes;
raising ice and oranges, fish and fossils, gold and anthra-
cite, — with its bowels full of oil for lights, coal for fuel,
gold for currency, iron and lead for the useful arts;
with prairies for wheat, interval for corn, hills for lum-
ber, plains for cotton, delta for sugar, mountains for
sheep, and meadows for cattle. Everything that a
great nation needs, that nature can furnish, is at our

service when the rebellion is subdued, and labor triumphs over idleness.

When the war is over, and the last battle won, the nation will arise with renewed energy, and stretch forth its arms with fresh vigor. It will make more rapid strides than ever toward wealth and power; and then, more than ever, we must guard the rights of the people against the encroachments of monopoly and combination. Every true democrat will then have duties and responsibilities requiring all the powers of mind and heart.

When I write this the contest is not over, and the battle still rages; but before it is much read it will be over, and, I have the fullest confidence, will end in the triumph of democracy, I hope over the whole, and all, opposition. I have no hope or confidence in the clergy to accomplish it, for they and our Christianity are on both sides, and prayers are as plenty, and earnest, and sincere, on the wrong as on the right side. Nor have I any hope in the providence usually relied on by Christians; for it is evidently a careless providence, that as often favors tyrants and aristocrats as laborers and democrats. Nor am I sure that the right always triumphs over the wrong, for I have repeatedly found the sentiment to be true, temporarily, that

"Sometimes have the better men
Through guile of worse supplanted been."

But I have the fullest confidence that the principles themselves have the power to triumph over all obstacles, and ultimately to build and bring up the working classes to the condition of wealth to and for all.

Next, after this contest is over, comes the great mission of democracy,—to emancipate and enfranchise woman, and place her on an equal footing with man in land, labor and education, that she may take equal part in politics and religion, in voting, preaching, pleading, and healing diseases of body and soul.

There is abundant work for reformers. When one point is gained, others are to gain. For ages the masses of the people have been robbed of nearly all their rights, and democracy is slowly restoring them to a few at a time, and but "a little at a time," though not "always of the prime."

Tyrants always refer to the French Revolution to prove that the people are not capable of self-government; and that, written by the aristocrats themselves and for their purposes, makes quite a good proof of the incapacity of the people everywhere while it is in the hands of enemies. Let the laborers everywhere unite and demand their rights to land, and education for their children,— for *all* children,— and let all train their children to a moderate amount of labor, and our country will soon lead the world, and control all nations for their advancement. Then right shall triumph over wrong and might.

The war of the Revolution was fought to secure the right of self-government by the people of the colonies, and to escape from tyranny and taxation by foreigners and aristocrats. The war of 1812 was fought to secure equal rights and jurisdiction on the ocean, and for our seamen; and both were successful because the hearts of a partially free and laboring people were engaged in them. The war of 1861 and '62 is fought by the people of the loyal States to secure the rights of all to land, labor and education, and the right of all to pursue and secure happiness with and under natural rights;

—free land, free labor, free schools, free homes, free hands, free hearts, free speech, free press, free pulpit, in all parts and places where the United States has jurisdiction; and whatever authority or institution is in the way of it *must* be removed, quietly if it can, forcibly if it must. Slavery, land monopoly, usury, banking monopolies, sectarian and partial religion and salvation, monarchy in heaven, and religion as on earth, must yield, and a democratic God have the place of the King of kings and Lord of lords. Individualism, rationalism and spiritualism will be triumphant "in the good time coming." Work "a little longer;" you need not wait, for " God works in the working soul, and helps those who help themselves."

It has not been my object, in this treatise, to point out the mistakes, weakness or wickedness of military or political leaders in this rebellion, although aware of many; for I also know that history will in the end do ample justice to each, and that these cannot singly or combinedly materially change the great issues or the final result; for it is certain that aristocracy must be greatly reduced and limited in its power and influence in the country, and slavery so crippled, and its advocates and upholders so disgraced, that it must soon end, even if not by the military power annulled in the contest.

It is now certain that, when the war is over, and the soldiers again return to their homes to cultivate the land and carry on the shops, the poor will be more respected, better paid and better protected, than ever before, and wealth and aristocracy will fall in an equal proportion; and this will be a great gain to the country at large.

There need be no fear of too much labor, black or white; for the soil and resources are ample for all, and happiness can be greatly increased for the many.  This is the working man's country, and his government, and he must maintain it and defend it, and it will shelter and protect him, and release him from slavery, poverty, ignorance, vice and misery.

www.ingramcontent.com/pod-product-compliance
Lightning Source LLC
Chambersburg PA
CBHW032357020726
47499CB00008B/2796